For Phil – NM

First published in Great Britain in 2002 by
Pavilion Children's Books
An imprint of Chrysalis Books plc
64 Brewery Road
London N7 9NT
www.pavilionbooks.co.uk

Designed by Sarah Goodwin

A CIP catalogue record for this book is available
from the British Library.

ISBN 1 84365 000 2

Set in Sabon
Printed by Imago Singapore

2 4 6 8 10 9 7 5 3 1

This book can be ordered direct from the publisher. Please contact
the Marketing Department. But try your bookshop first.

Mouse Tells the Time

Nicola Moon
Illustrated by Anthony Morris

"How do you tell the time?"
Mouse asked Hedgehog one day.

"I look up at the sky," said Hedgehog.
"If it's light, it's day, and if it's dark, it's night."
"Is that all?" said Mouse.
"It's enough," said Hedgehog, shuffling off
 into the undergrowth.

But it wasn't enough for Mouse.
"I already know that!" he said to himself.
"I want to know more."
He went to find Squirrel.
Squirrel always seemed to know everything.
He soon found him, busily gathering acorns
under the old oak tree.

"How do you tell the time?" Mouse asked Squirrel.

"Shadows," said Squirrel.

"Shadows?" said Mouse.

"Long shadows pointing west, it's morning.
Long shadows pointing east, it's evening.
Little short shadows, it's midday."

"What if there are no shadows?" asked Mouse.

"Then the sun isn't shining," said Squirrel,
darting up the tree.

Mouse looked at his shadow.
It didn't seem to be very long,
but it wasn't very short either.
And he had no idea which was east
and which was west.
Then the sun went behind a cloud
and he couldn't see his shadow at all.
There must be an easier way to tell the time!

"How do you tell the time?"
  Mouse asked the Rabbit twins.
"With dandelion clocks," said the Rabbits.
"Show me how," said Mouse.
"One blow and it's one o' clock,"
  said Brother Rabbit.
"Two blows and it's two o' clock,"
  said Sister Rabbit.

"So what time is it now?" asked Mouse.

"Six o' clock!" puffed Sister Rabbit, bounding
off across the field.

"Thirteen o' clock!" panted Brother Rabbit,
scampering after his sister.

Mouse felt more confused than ever. He knew
it couldn't be six o' clock *and* thirteen o' clock.
He wasn't even sure there *was* a thirteen o' clock,
and now he had a dandelion seed stuck in his ear.
He decided to go and find Grandma Mole.
Grandma Mole was very wise.

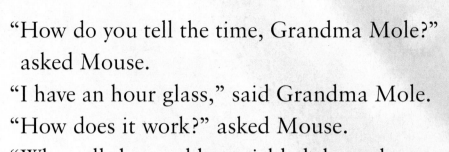

"How do you tell the time, Grandma Mole?"
   asked Mouse.
"I have an hour glass," said Grandma Mole.
"How does it work?" asked Mouse.
"When all the sand has trickled through
   the little hole it means one hour has gone by,"
   said Grandma Mole.

"So what time is it now?" asked Mouse.
"One hour later than it was before," said
   Grandma Mole, and popped down her hole.

Mouse now felt completely baffled,
and he still didn't know how to tell the time.
He was also beginning to feel rather hungry,
so he decided to go home.

"Telling the time is very complicated," Mouse told
  Mother when he got home.
"Not really," said Mother. "Are you hungry?"
"Starving!" said Mouse.
"Then it must be supper time," said Mother.

After supper Mouse gave an enormous yawn.
"Now I think it must be bedtime,"
  laughed Mother.
"And when I wake up in the morning,
  it will be getting-up time!" said Mouse.
"But what if I want to know all
  the in-between times?
  What if I want to tell the time for real,
  with numbers?"

"Then you have to look at a clock," said Mother.

"Show me," said Mouse.

"Tomorrow," promised Mother.

"It's a long time until tomorrow," complained
Mouse.

"Not if you close your eyes," said Mother,
kissing him goodnight.

Mouse snuggled down in bed and closed his eyes.
In no time at all he was fast asleep
and dreaming of tomorrow,
the day when he would learn
how to tell the time.

Three o' clock
Playtime

Five o' clock
Supper time

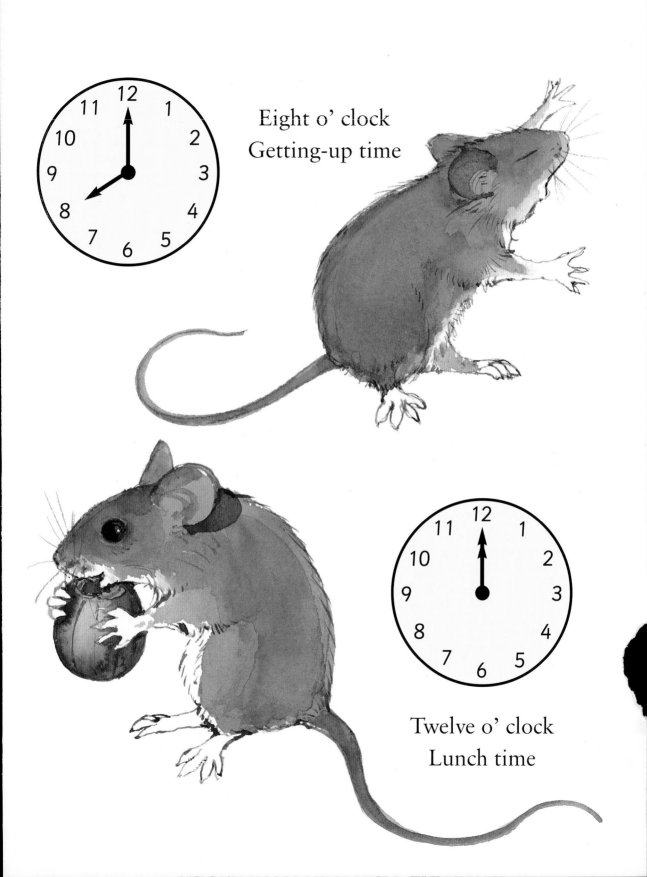

Eight o' clock
Getting-up time

Twelve o' clock
Lunch time